STELLAR POSSIBILITIES

by John J. Dunphy

illustrations by 7ARS

Stellar Possibilities
by John J. Dunphy

All rights reserved. No part of this book may be reproduced or transmitted in any form or by any means, electronic or mechanical, including photocopying or recording or by any information storage and retrieval systems, without expressed written consent of the author and/or artists.

Stellar Possibilities is a work of fiction. Names, characters, places, and incidents are products of the author's imagination. Any resemblance to actual events or persons, living or dead, is entirely coincidental.

Poem copyrights owned by John J. Dunphy

Cover illustration "Stellar Passions" © 2016 by Mitchell Davidson Bentley

Cover design by Laura Givens

First Printing, January 2016
Second Printing, March 2024

Hiraeth Publishing
P.O. Box 1248
Tularosa, NM 88352
e-mail: hiraethsubs@yahoo.com

Visit www.hiraethsffh.com for science fiction, fantasy, dark fiction, and more. **Support the small, independent press...**

For Aunt Dot and Uncle Joe, who made my life possible.

Acknowledgements:

Some of the material contained herein was previously published in Scifaikuest, Raw Nervz Haiku, Frogpond, Brussels Sprout, and The Shantytown Anomaly.

Illustrations by 7ARS

Contents

7   scifaiku

28   haibun

39   more scifaiku

the alien's language
lacking a word
for war

the Count's Halloween party
guests gasp in horror at
his paintings of sunrises

32 straight sevens
the telekinetic alien
shoots craps

fast-food restaurant
long line of spaceships hover
in the drive-thru lane

preparing to land
the blue-green planet below
so much like Old Earth

the alien tourist
his ten-gallon hat on
a 20-gallon head

meteor shower
even more stunning seen from
another planet

alien envoy
extends his limb in greeting
I try to shake hands

in the museum
of ancient technology
a plastic slide rule

engineer's cabin
hologram of his sweetheart
hovers by the bed

first space assignment
in the ensign's desk drawer
a worn rabbit's foot

our stop-over at
the galactic tourist trap
cheap space junk galore

communion
the alien convert receives a host
on each tongue

used spaceship lot
dealer rolls back an odometer
800 million miles

cemetery
where once Dad's tombstone stood
his hologram

first interplanetary colonists
in each person's belongings
a canister of earth

baptismal water
on the alien infant's forehead
sizzling

a flasher!
the alien tourist covers
her child's eye

low-rent alien housing
in front of one trailer
pink humans

another checkmate
I glare across the board at
my chuckling android

nightfall on Tansen
child learning his numbers counts
moons on his fingers

Halloween party
my incognito alien friend
wins "best costume"

Peace Corps training program
I request an assignment
on another planet

jury selection
prosecutor objects to
the defendant's clone

my face on a wanted poster -
I cringe upon reading
my clone's latest crimes

picket line
strikers shout threats at
the android scabs

open season
young hunter poses beside
his first human

summer solstice
dew-dampened finger anoints
her infant daughter

six months pregnant
she walks through the orchard
touching each tree

Holocaust Museum
an alien visitor asks to borrow
one of my tears

ex-nuclear test site
a prairie dog peers from its hole
with both heads

Vietnam Veterans Memorial
an alien tourist comforts
a weeping Earthling

school cafeteria
the half-alien child
eats alone

child's burial
weeping next to the parents
the android nanny

prom night
her alien date's boutonniere
growing from his chest

Miss Galaxy Pageant
the Tansen contestant shows cleavage
from eight breasts

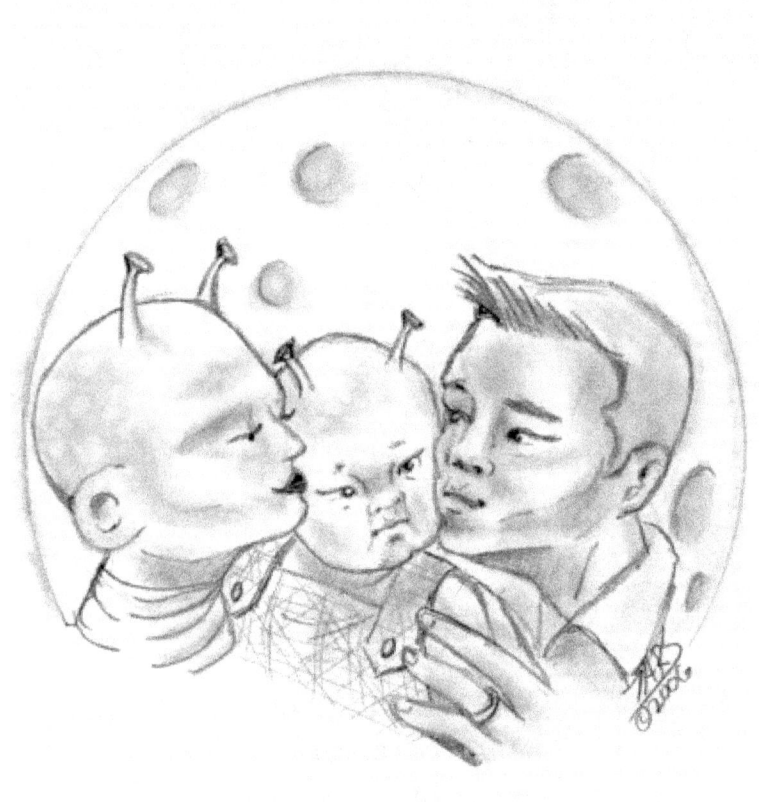

alien wedding
the bride and groom join hands
and hands and hands

their make-out planet
the alien teens' parked spaceships form
more crop circles

his turn to bowl -
the alien rolls a ball
in every lane

Mardi Gras
a drunken alien bares
her 26 breasts

Indy 500
an alien competes
on foot

experimental laboratory
two caged subjects discover
they both speak English

VFW Post
special induction rite for
the first Planetary War veteran

Earth-Tansen Treaty Talks
the alien diplomat lying
out of each mouth

Earth
the alien hitchhiker's thumb
pointed upward

my first teleportation
engineer laughs when I materialize
with crossed fingers

Pledge of Allegiance
the alien immigrant covers
both his hearts

pleasure planet
the alien offers to massage me with
all eight hands

alien nightclub
the lounge lizard
a lizard

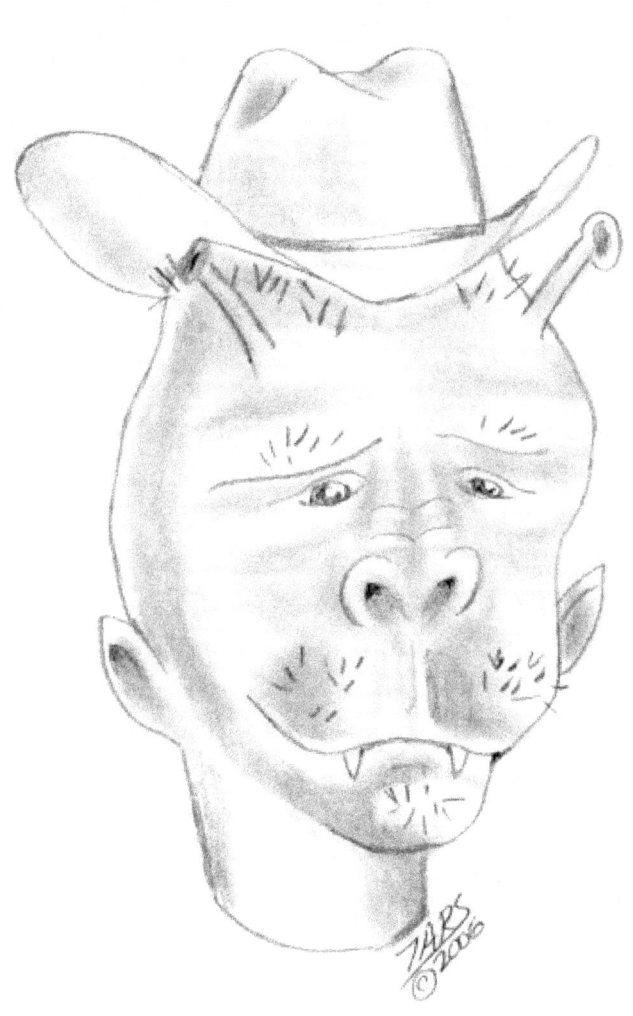

A Horror of Old

"Places like this littered our Earth in centuries past. Humanity had no recourse except to warehouse certain people, since even the most sophisticated forms of behavioral modification -- or therapy, to employ a term used at the time -- were only moderately successful at best.

"Genetic engineering empowered our species to minimize and eventually eliminate the tendencies that made institutions such as this a necessity for humanity's well-being. Those of you with psychic ability likely sense the residual emotions of hopelessness and rage that were encased in this building.

"We sometimes asked why our government has chosen to preserve such grim historical sites. Our leaders believe -- and I fully concur with them-- that humanity needs to be reminded about the naivety of romanticizing the past. Just imagine having to live in a civilization that included such horrors as this institution."

    the tour guide's lecture
    as we walk though
    a prison

The Bookworm's Vacation

The guy at the Time Travel Recreation Company assured me that it would be the ideal vacation for a bibliophile such as myself. I was a bit skeptical at first. After all, this was the same company that promised me I'd have the time of my life at Woodstock. Yeah, I got to hear some classic rock groups, but the site was a rain-soaked muddy mess -- not to mention the bad acid. But *this* trip was the experience of a lifetime.

Never -- and I mean *never* -- have I been at a place that contained so much fascinating reading material. At first I had trouble perusing it because my eyes kept misting up with tears. Yes, I was that happy. I've recommended this vacation to all my friends who love books.

> a lost dialogue of Plato!
> I find another treasure in
> the library of Alexandria

Shipwrecked

Opportunities in New York City seemed rather limited for a chap with my kind of ambition, so I decided to seek my fortune prospecting for gold in California. I had heard that one could pluck half-pound gold nuggets from its streams and make millions of dollars in just a few days. Accordingly, I boarded a ship that would sail around the tip of South America and then up to the California coast.

We encountered a fearful storm somewhere off the coast of Brazil, and our ship went down. Never a strong swimmer, I was flailing about in the water when a coffin suddenly surfaced. It must have been part of the ship's cargo. I swam to it with my last ounce of strength and grasped it for dear life.

I, apparently the sole survivor of this catastrophe, cling to a coffin that floats in the South Atlantic Ocean without hope of discovery and rescue. Could my plight possibly be more pitiful?

>dusk --
>the coffin's lid
>springs open

The Tattoo Freak

    I'm a guy who digs tattoos. My arms, back and chest are crammed with them. And we're not talking cheap junk or jailhouse tattoos here. This beach boy's body is a canvas for work by some of the most distinguished masters of the art of tattoo. None of the women I've dated have given me any grief over my tattoos -- until now, that is.
    Phyllis likes to think of herself as a high-society chick and acts like it."Bob," she'll say as we walk along the beach, "you'd be a handsome man if only you hadn't desecrated your body with those horrible things." If I've heard that from her once, I've heard it a hundred times. Phyllis hates my tattoos, so tonight I'm going to lose them just for her. I bet she likes my body even less without them.

> full moon beachwalk
> her boyfriend's tattoos
> now covered with fur

The Backwoods Patriot

I can find underground water, just like my daddy and his daddy before him -- all the way back for generations. Some folks call it dowsing, but I like to call it water witching.

It's a gift that comes in useful when somebody here in eastern Kentucky needs to dig a new well. I just hold my divining rod with both hands and walk around until the rod starts twitching and points down. And, sure enough, that's where the water always is!

I was milking my cows when this string of long black cars pulled up. Some men wearing suits and other men wearing uniforms got out and said that my country needed me. "Hey, boys," I said, "if you all got a war goin' on, I'm a sure-shot but way too old for 20-mile hikes carryin' all that equipment!" You could have knocked me over with a feather when they said that the government knew all about my water witching and I was needed to find some water for Uncle Sam. Well, I love this country, so I said, "Sure thing, boys! Just take me where you need me!"

Me and my big mouth. Well, the sooner I find water, the sooner them government big-shots will take me back home.

    water witch
    walks across
    the lunar landscape

The New Multi-Lingualism

In the United States of the nineteenth-century, learning a foreign language in high school meant studying Greek or Latin. Twentieth-century educators realized the importance of learning modern foreign languages, so students began taking classes in French, German and Spanish. Beginning in the first decade of the twenty-first century, classes in sign language could be taken to satisfy foreign-language requirements.

Ultimately, it's all about becoming more proficient in communicating with other people, right? That's why a few far-sighted educators, such as myself, began pushing for yet another way to allow gifted high school students to satisfy the foreign language requirement. Conservative school board members and many principals continue to fight us tooth and nail, but every academic year sees yet another high school adding these courses to its curriculum. I firmly believe that our society can only benefit by helping young people develop yet another way to communicate.

class registration --
a student signs up for
first-year telepathy

A King of Old Earth

Many inhabitants of my planet applaud the achievements of past Earthlings who excelled in science. I, however, am alone in revering this Earthling, who was a giant in a field other than science. In my opinion, his influence in shaping and defining Earth civilization was no less trailblazing than that of Copernicus and Einstein.

I believe that this human's greatness will someday be recognized by others of my kind. Until that time, this extraterrestial will pay homage to him in the company of his fellow Earthlings.

    an alien
    in the line to visit
    Elvis's grave

The Convert

Many inhabitants of my planet were astounded when I so readily embraced one of the Earth's religions. But it really wasn't a conversion so much as it was the discovery of a religion that embodied so many of the beliefs that I had always held.

This Earth religion brought me such joy that I became as member of its clergy. I rose through its ranks over the measure of time that Earthlings call decades. Last year, a select group of my co-religionists chose me as the supreme leader of this faith's largest branch. I am the first of my kind to attain this post, which only serves to prove that this wonderful religion is truly universal. It was difficult for some Earthlings to accept me. Now, however, they not only accept me but love me as much as I love them.

St. Peter's Square --
parents lift their child to see
the first alien pope

The Illegal

I'm not an animal, but I know all too well what it's like to be hunted.

I am an illegal immigrant. I came here to escape poverty and make a better life for myself. Some politicians claim that I steal jobs from decent, hard-working people like you. Let me say that this accusation is totally untrue. Like other illegal immigrants, I work low-paying jobs that you would turn up your noses at: scrubbing public toilets; migratory farm work; hazardous waste clean-up...you name the dirty, dangerous job and I've probably done it.

I'm currently washing dishes during the nightshift in a disgusting greasy spoon. You probably would never eat at a place like this, let alone work here. Well, I work here -- and in constant fear that police and immigration authorities will arrest and deport me.

    all-nite cafe
    an illegal washes dishes
    with all four hands

Compassion

I was conducting a reconnaissance mission over a planet whose inhabitants have barely advanced beyond the discovery of fire and the wheel. I detected a large group of them making their way across a particularly desolate stretch of land that contained limited food and water.

My mission commander has repeatedly cautioned me about aiding primitive species. If they are to develop a civilization, then it must be through their own efforts in order to ensure that the civilization is truly indigenous, rather than merely an extension of an alien culture. While I agree with this directive and generally observe it, there are times when it *must* be violated. I believed that this was one of those times.

Those poor creatures were starving. I hovered far above them and released some emergency rations to keep them alive until they located other resources. I sometimes wonder how they rationalized the sudden appearance of food.

Sinai desert
Hebrews gather
their daily manna

my new Entrance Security System
a door-to-door salesman
caught in its spam filter

historical reenactment
an engineer wearing glasses uses
a slide rule

veterans' hospital
two patients compete
to see who can
more quickly grow
a new limb

genetically-modified forest
a tree-hugger
hugged back

near-sighted
my ophthalmologist suggests
new eyes

wormhole entrance
commuter tosses change at
the toll booth attendant

first alien guest
hotel handyman lowers
the bathroom mirror

Museum of Alien Religions
visitors gape at
a crucifix

memory implant store
a wannabe is now haunted
by combat flashbacks

the expanding universe --
my alien lover and I
growing farther apart

museum of ancient technology
my child asks about
the gas pump

quantum vacation
the numbers on our hotel room
keep changing

car wreck
the dead man survives
in a parallel universe

archaeological exploration
painted on a cave wall
mushroom clouds

getting old
first bifocals and hearing aid
for my dog

Christmas Eve
I set our yard's weather selector
for snow

kidney transplant
I write a thank-you note
to my clone

Midwest excavation
an alien skeleton riddled with
stone arrowheads

new yard-control app
I set the lawn
for two-inch grass

polygamist
each wife and family in
a parallel universe

no insects yet --
the flower
changes color

putting down roots
I congratulate an alien immigrant upon
his new rhizome

first alien centerfold
readers ogle her legs
and legs and legs

zero-gravity lovemaking
who's on top
keeps changing

Global Warming Triptych

Africa
wind-blown dust from
the lake bed

Museum of Extinct Species
my child points at
the polar bear

2165 C.E.
divers explore
Miami

alien immigrant family
another cross set afire
in their front yard

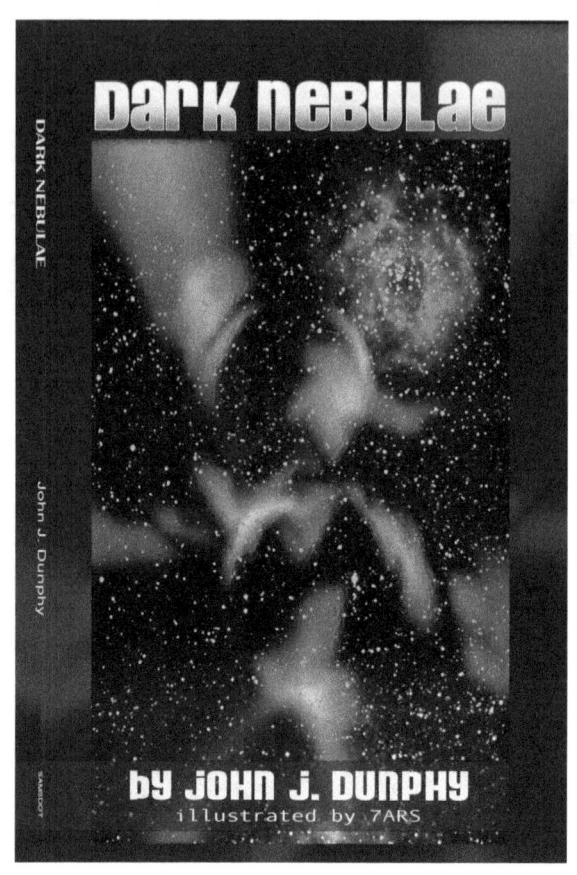

Dark Nebulae
https://www.hiraethsffh.com/product-page/dark-nebulae-by-john-j-dunphy

Go. Now.

www.ingramcontent.com/pod-product-compliance
Lightning Source LLC
LaVergne TN
LVHW051925060526
838201LV00062B/4695